HEAT

Helen Ketteman

Illustrations by Scott Goto

WALKER & COMPANY
New York

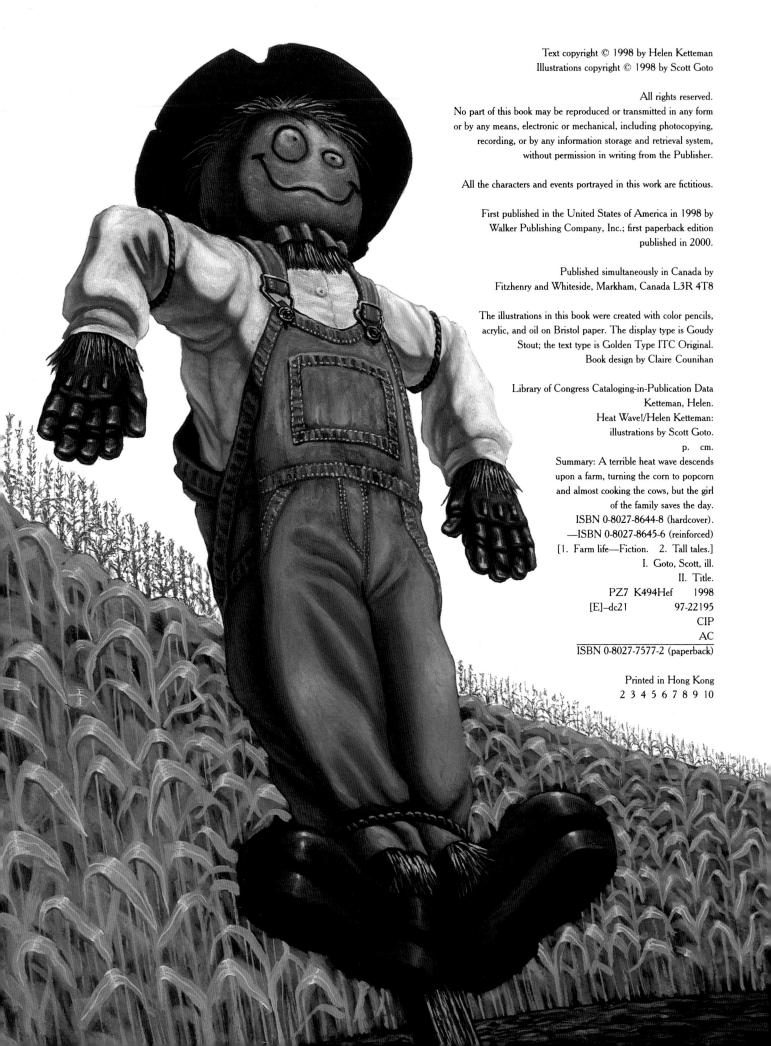

Text copyright © 1998 by Helen Ketteman
Illustrations copyright © 1998 by Scott Goto

First published in the United States of America in 1998 by
Walker Publishing Company, Inc.; first paperback edition
published in 2000.

Published simultaneously in Canada by
Fitzhenry and Whiteside, Markham, Canada L3R 4T8

The illustrations in this book were created with color pencils,
acrylic, and oil on Bristol paper. The display type is Goudy
Stout; the text type is Golden Type ITC Original.
Book design by Claire Counihan

Library of Congress Cataloging-in-Publication Data
Ketteman, Helen.
Heat Wave!/Helen Ketteman:
illustrations by Scott Goto.
p. cm.
Summary: A terrible heat wave descends
upon a farm, turning the corn to popcorn
and almost cooking the cows, but the girl
of the family saves the day.
ISBN 0-8027-8644-8 (hardcover).
—ISBN 0-8027-8645-6 (reinforced)
[1. Farm life—Fiction.   2. Tall tales.]
I. Goto, Scott, ill.
II. Title.
PZ7 K494Hef   1998
[E]–dc21   97-22195
CIP
AC
ISBN 0-8027-7577-2 (paperback)

Printed in Hong Kong
2 3 4 5 6 7 8 9 10

To my Texas critique group:
Carol, Chris, Diane, Ed,
and Jane.

        —H. K.

For Jiro and Doris Kawahara
and Aleix.

        —S. G.

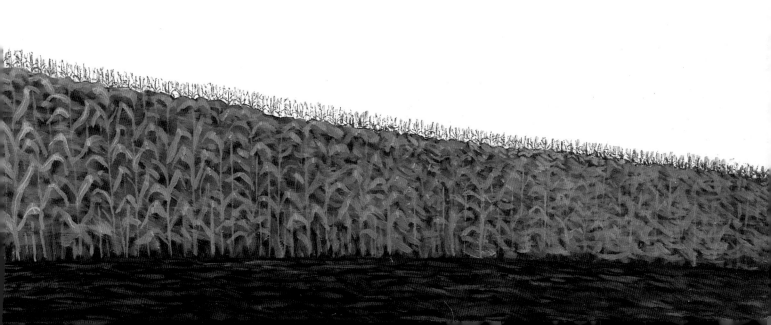

My big brother, Hank, used to tease me that girls couldn't be farmers. But he sure changed his tune the day the Heat Wave hit.

I was feeding the chickens when I heard a loud roar. I looked out across the horizon and saw a big old clump of crinkled, yellow air rolling across the sky. A flock of geese flew in one side and came out the other side plucked, stuffed, and roasted.

I hollered for Ma and Pa and Hank, but before they got outside, the Heat Wave hit. The mercury blasted out of the porch thermometer like a rocket. Ma's flowers pulled themselves up by their roots and crawled under the porch looking for shade.

By the time everybody ran outside, the Heat Wave had gotten snagged on the barn's weather vane. It was near harvest time, so we raced to the cornfield to save what we could. But by the time we got there, it was already too late. The corn had started popping. It looked like a blizzard had hit. One of our old hound dogs turned blue and froze when he saw it. I wrapped him in a blanket, and he thawed out okay.

Then we heard a commotion in the pasture. We raced over. The cows were hopping around like rabbits. The ground had gotten too hot, so we herded them inside the barn. They still looked miserable, though. Pa figured their milk had gotten too hot, so we set to milking. As it turned out, the cows had jumped so much, they'd churned their milk to butter. It came out melted. We'd milked the last of the butter when I had an idea.

We scrubbed a couple of shovels and the beds of the pickup trucks, then I sent Pa and Hank to the field to fill the pickups with popcorn.

When they were done, they brought the trucks around, and we all pitched in and poured the butter over the popcorn. Then Hank and Ma drove the trucks to the drive-in movie down the road. In no time at all, they sold every last bit of that popcorn, then hurried home.

We still had plenty of worries. We hurried to the field where we had oats planted. Sure enough, they had dried out. I tried wetting them down, but that didn't turn out to be such a good idea.

Soon I felt something slimy and thick rising up around my ankles. In another minute, it was waist high, and I could barely move. Turned out I'd created a whole field of oatmeal. It was lumpy, just like Ma's, and I about drowned in the stuff.

I dog-paddled to the edge and crawled out. Whoo-ee! That oatmeal was sticky! I told Pa we should bottle it, which we did later. It made fine glue.

It was then that I caught a whiff of something burning. I followed my nose to the barn and hurried inside. The cows were steaming, and their coats were starting to singe. Those poor critters were about to cook! We hosed them down and turned fans on them. It helped, but not enough. Pa always said I was the quickest thinker in the family, and I knew it was up to me to think of something else.

I figured it was time to take on the Heat Wave. I thought blowing air on it would help, but we needed the fans for the cows. Besides, we didn't have near enough fans to cool the Heat Wave down. Then I had another idea. A huge flock of crows, all beating their wings at once, might work. One thing Kansas has is plenty of crows. And I knew how to get them to come.

We dumped several fifty-pound bags of flour and a bunch of yeast in the trough by the barn, then stirred in water with shovels. That dough rose so fast we had to run for our lives. It rolled over several chickens, then picked up the tractor and Sally the mule. Ended up big as the barn.

A few minutes later, the dough started baking in the heat. Smelled awful good, and that's what I was counting on. Crows can't resist the smell of baking bread, and soon every crow in Kansas came flocking to the farm. Their wings made so much wind, we had to tie ourselves around a giant tree trunk to keep from being blown away. It felt cooler already.

The trouble was, those crows didn't keep flying. They lit on the bread and started eating. The temperature shot right back up, and I figured we might be licked.

The crows pecked at the bread until they freed Sally and the chickens. None of them were a bit worse for wear. In fact, they were right frisky. I figured all that yeast had caused their spirits to rise.

Seeing Sally gave me one more idea. I told Pa to hitch her to the plow, and she plowed up a section of land in record time. While Pa was plowing, I found what I needed. I gave everyone lettuce seeds, and we started planting. Those seeds sprouted as soon as they hit the dirt.

The bigger the lettuce grew, the cooler the air got. That Heat Wave put up a fight, all right. It rippled and twisted and squirmed like a bucking bronco. But as the lettuce cooled the air more, the Heat Wave started shrinking, until it finally disappeared altogether.

The weather vane and the barn cooled down, and the cows stopped steaming, too. They didn't seem much affected, except the fuzz on their hides never grew back. Ma had to knit them all sweaters for the winter.

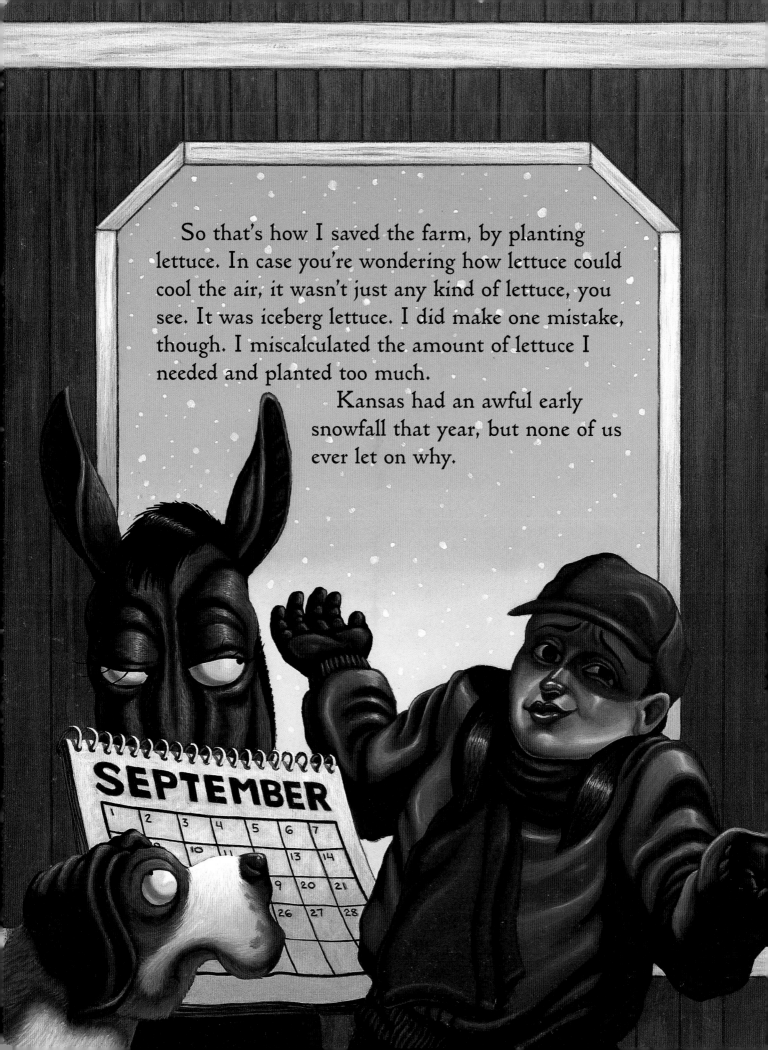

So that's how I saved the farm, by planting lettuce. In case you're wondering how lettuce could cool the air, it wasn't just any kind of lettuce, you see. It was iceberg lettuce. I did make one mistake, though. I miscalculated the amount of lettuce I needed and planted too much.

Kansas had an awful early snowfall that year, but none of us ever let on why.

SEPTEMBER